T0065233

HOMEGOING

Stories, Poems and Dreams

SUSAN KNIER

"The quality of mercy is not strained. It droppeth as the gentle rain from heaven upon the place beneath. It is twice blessed – It blesseth him that gives and him that takes."

William Shakespeare

HOMEGOING
STORIES, POEMS AND DREAMS

iUniverse books may be ordered through booksellers or by contacting:

iUniverse
1663 Liberty Drive
Bloomington, IN 47403
www.iuniverse.com
844-349-9409

ISBN: 978-1-6632-1517-8 (sc)
ISBN: 978-1-6632-1518-5 (e)

Print information available on the last page.

iUniverse rev. date: 12/21/2020

STORIES

LA SALSA

"You really need to get out more. You're practically married to your job!" It was my friend Dory who worked as an RN at Methodist Hospital. She and I were college buddies and coincidentally took jobs in the same city after graduation. Lately, she was also my only friend given my long hours as a salaried CPA in a small accounting firm in a dingy office in an industrial park just outside of downtown. A very small firm indeed – just myself and the boss, a dour, perplexed man named Joe who always seemed to be saying "What?" and scratching his balding head.

Dory's sigh rasped through the phone at my silence. "You know, I go back to second shift next week but I'm on days all this week. We should go out to dinner! There's a new Mexican place on Fremont. The owner is a psychiatrist I used to work with at Methodist."

I was intrigued. "No kidding," I said. The thought of personal transformation in my current tired, burned-out state seemed remarkable.

"Yeah. He's Dr. Jaime Guerrero. He retired suddenly last year and without a word to anyone at the hospital he started this restaurant."

"What's it called?"

"La Salsa. How about I pick you up at 7:00?"

I hesitated, looking at my littered desk. I could easily work again until midnight and chew on another lukewarm microwave pizza in bed but this sounded infinitely better. Maybe it was just what I needed. I said yes.

Mexican polka music echoed from the speakers above as the hostess led us to a table with two enormous wicker chairs. Colored lights crisscrossed the ceiling. Before I knew it, Dory and I were grasping cold, sweaty margaritas. I reached for a chip and dipped it in a large gob of salsa.

"Hey, there he is!" Dory gestured excitedly over my shoulder.

I turned to see a man of about sixty speaking solemnly to our server. He wore the traditional white culinary tunic and pants with an immaculate apron around his waist. His broad mustache creased into dimples as he smiled in our direction. He was on his way to our table, carrying a bowl of something.

"Good evening, ladies," he intoned, nodding to each of us.

"Dr. Guerrero!" gushed Dory. "Hello!"

"Please call me Jaime. Dr. Guerrero is ancient history," he laughed. ("Is" sounded like "eees" in his strong Mexican accent). Jaime's attention turned to the small bowl he was holding. "I apologize for the error. You were given the wrong salsa." He proceeded to exchange the bowls of salsa. "You should really have this one," he reinforced as he gently placed the bowl in front of us. ("This" sounded like "theees").

"Oh, thank you!" I said. "But the first salsa was fine."

Jaime's face darkened as if I had proffered an insult. "This one is my great grandmother's authentic recipe from Jalisco." He clasped his hands together in a prayerlike stance. "It will make you wiser."

At that moment, I looked into Jaime's eyes. They were dark around the edges but two light brown "tunnels" were evident in the center. Maybe it was just the lighting. I felt myself looking deeper into his eyes as if I couldn't look away.

"Well," Jaime clapped his hands together. "Do enjoy yourselves." And he turned gracefully on his heel and left our table.

"That was weird," Dory said slowly.

"He's a …powerful person, isn't he?"

Dory shrugged. "I need another one," she said nonchalantly, hoisting an empty margarita glass.

The "new" salsa was wonderful, for lack of an original word. My tongue appreciated cilantro and several spices I could not immediately name, but it worked well with the obviously homemade chips.

"You keep eating all those chips and salsa and you won't eat your meal," reminded Dory.

"Right!" I replied, mouth full. I thought of the seafood enchiladas that were upcoming – no doubt another authentic recipe from Jaime's great grandmother…

After dinner (and how sumptuous it was!), Dory and I lazily visited at the table as our food comas approached.

"You know, you work way too hard!" Dory said. "Being salaried seems like a legal form of slavery to me."

Dory was right. Joe was "flexible" in that I could make my own schedule as long as the work was done on time. But it was simply too much.

"Is Joe going to hire you an associate?"

"It's not in the works yet, but I'll bring it up at my performance review. He's got to see that I'm overworked."

Dory leaned toward me. "Exactly!" she hissed angrily. "He knows you need help but he will keep you going twenty hours a day because it's cheaper than adding staff! What if you drop dead on the job?"

I scoffed. "C'mon, Dory. Hard work doesn't kill you."

"Oh yeah? Hello! I'm the nurse here! Overwork and strong emotional stress can lead to cardiovascular complications, CVAs, mental and behavioral health issues-"

Her laundry list of medical maladies was interrupted by the server politely delivering the check.

I slept better than I had in months – maybe since graduation. Maybe Dory was right. I truly needed more "work-life balance" if I wanted to survive and thrive. As I dressed for work, I vowed to ask Joe for more help. I was kidding myself that this was a "career" job. I didn't want to be a "lifer" in a small time accounting office in a drab industrial park anyway. I was made for better things.

So courage was top of mind as I logged onto my desktop at work. I felt so clear and refreshed. Maybe it was the two margaritas, I laughed to myself. Ancient Jalisco recipe! I actually chuckled aloud at that. I glanced into Joe's office. He was frowning and absently scratching his head. His swivel chair creaked as he leaned back. I waved good morning to him and commenced my work.

11:49 AM. Yes, 11:49 AM. Not 11:49 PM (or 2:07 AM, like last week Thursday). My heart quickened. My work was completely done and it wasn't even noon! How could this be? I didn't quite understand it as I knocked on the door of Joe's office.

"Yuh?" he replied, immediately reaching up to scratch his cranium.

"Uh, Joe, I'm done."

"What? Quitting?"

"No, Joe. I'm done with all of today's accounts."

He wordlessly brushed past me to my desktop. I hadn't signed out yet, anticipating scrutiny. He scrolled through my work, murmuring a periodic "Well, I'll be" or "Damn!"

"Okay, you can go," Joe said, hiking up his pants. "Uh, see ya' tomorrow?"

"Okay," I said, purse already on my shoulder and body turned toward the door.

In the car, I texted Dory. Texting a busy RN was a hit-or-miss proposition, but Dory replied within ten minutes.

ME: I'm done with work! How about La Salsa tonight? 6:00? 7:00?

DORY: WTF! Fired? Quit?

ME: No, just efficient today. Dinner at La Salsa?

DORY: OK, I guess I could try a mole dish. 7:00.

After a long nap at home, I headed over to La Salsa for Happy Hour. No chips/salsa, just a margarita that I nursed for 90 minutes prior to Dory's arrival. Dory came through the door at 6:55 and we were promptly seated at the same table in those capacious wicker chairs. We had the same server, finding out tonight that her name was Hortencia. She promptly brought two frozen margaritas, the homemade chips and…the heavenly salsa. I immediately plowed a chip into a generous glob of salsa as we placed our orders.

"Is Jaime here tonight?" I asked, casually loading up another chip.

"He can't be here every night," interjected Dory.

"Oh, yes, he is here," said Hortencia as she recorded our orders. "He is in the back making salsa. He was very disappointed in me last night because I served you a canned salsa. We ran out of the right salsa. He wanted you to have it!" Hortencia looked at me and clasped her hands to her chest. "Lo siento mucho. I am very sorry."

I was already loading up another chip with salsa. "Nothing to apologize for," I said absently. I noticed a perplexed look on Dory's face but she was silent.

After Hortencia left, there was a brief silence between Dory and I as I chewed.

"I'll be interested to see how chocolate sauce works with Mexican food," Dory finally said.

"Dory, I got 14 hours of work done in less than 4 hours today. I went home before noon!"

Dory froze. Finally she said, "What's going on?"

"I don't know. I'm just so sharp and on top of things. I think I'm going to go home and learn French tonight. I've always wanted to."

"What's wrong with you? Are you drunk?"

"No, I only had one margarita while I waited for you."

"Easy on the salsa, kid. You won't eat your dinner!"

"Okay, mom," I retorted, rolling my eyes. "Hey, Dory, maybe it's the salsa!" I held up a chip heavy with it toward her.

"What?!"

"Dory, did you notice any changes in yourself since having this salsa last night?"

"No, I was just a little cranky getting up for a shift that started at 6:30 AM, unlike you CPAs who start at midday…"

"Do you think we'll see Jaime tonight?"

Dory sighed in exasperation. "You are really fixated on him and that salsa. Girl, you're crushing on a guy that could be your grandfather!" She produced her cell phone. "We've got to get you out there on Tinder or Match.com or something!"

"It's just…those eyes of his!"

The evening passed in mole, more chips (and salsa) and conversation. I then went home and mastered the French language by 2:28 AM.

The next three weeks passed in super productive work days (average of two hours for a 14-20 hour workload). I also mastered Korean in an evening. I dined nightly at La Salsa, more often alone because of Dory's changing shifts and other excuses, including dates. I didn't care. Hortencia treated me like a daughter. My wicker chair and usual table were my castle. Eventually I stopped ordering dinner altogether and focused on consuming as many chips and particularly salsa as I reasonably could in an evening. Eventually I began ordering a small a-la-carte entrée to go because Hortencia told me that she was not allowed to pack up the remaining salsa to go. I would wait for her to leave and then surreptitiously pour it into my take-out container. One night, Hortencia delivered the salsa in a hand-painted bowl rimmed with pearls on the outside.

"This was Señor Guerrero's great grandmother's bowl. He wanted to serve you with it tonight," she said. I was touched and mesmerized by the exquisite bowl with the even more exquisite salsa brimming from it. One night, I stopped eating the chips and started simply drinking the salsa directly from the bowl – just as Joe sometimes consumed soup in his office. No one seemed to notice.

Speaking of Joe, my efficiency was so great that I was only working about ten hours a week. Thank God I was salaried or I would have needed four to five jobs to earn enough. I would certainly have the time, as I was suddenly thriving on about four hours of sleep a night.

One morning around 10:30 AM I was getting ready to leave for the day (ha!) when Joe waved me into his office.

"Alison?"

"Joe?"

"Have a seat."

We both sat. He scratched his head in silence as his chair again creaked.

He cleared his throat. "Well, Alison, I'd like to offer you a 3% raise. Your work, of late, has been incredibly, er, efficient."

I nearly scoffed. "Thank you," I managed.

"Okay, then. See you tomorrow."

"Okay." I turned to leave but then Joe spoke again.

"Yeah, I had actually hired a guy, you know, part-time, to help you but I rescinded the offer because here you are – SUPERWOMAN!" He laughed in a shrill cackle.

I swallowed hard and left.

After a long nap, I mastered Spanish by dinnertime. I was so excited. I could now conduct all of my business at La Salsa in the native tongue. As I walked up to the restaurant at 7:00, I imagined a conversation in his native tongue with the elusive Jaime.

Oddly, no one was parked in the lot. I could see some of the overhead lights on, but most of the restaurant was in darkness. I approached the front door to read a handwritten sign:

> CLOSED
> VISITING FAMILY IN MEXICO
> THANK YOU FOR YOUR PATRONAGE!

My blood ran cold in my veins. What? Closed?! Why hadn't Hortencia said anything? I paced, contemplating my next move. I then saw a light on in the business next door, a check-cashing business. I ran in, startling a man with a graying man-bun.

"Sir, when is La Salsa back open?"

"What? Oh, I wouldn't know, ma'am. I barely know them. I'm just collecting their mail in the meantime."

"Well, then you MUST know when they'll be back. WHEN?" I was shouting.

"I – I don't know."

"They must have told you when they'd be back."

"No, ma'am. Now listen-"

"Well, how long are they usually gone when they visit family?" I was squealing in a desperate tone.

A sheen of sweat shone on the man's alarmed face. "I don't know – maybe a month or so?"

"A month?!" I was completely shattered. "Do you have Dr. Guerrero's - Jaime's – contact information?"

"Ma'am, I can't give you that!"

I was short-circuiting with fear and anxiety as I ran back out into the night.

My brain felt like frozen mud at work the next day. At 5:00, Joe sidled up to my chaotic desk. "Still workin', huh?"

I blinked desperately at him.

"Uh, see you tomorrow," he said, shrugging.

I knew right then what I had to do.

Dory was on second shift at Methodist Hospital. She had said something about working in ortho that week. I ran past the COVID-19 checkpoint table as the attendant dialed security. I knew I was on borrowed time at best.

I found Dory on the fourth floor, talking quietly to a colleague in the hallway. As I called her name, she did a double take and then ran toward me, taking me into an empty patient room. I was crying and disjointedly telling her about La Salsa being closed.

Dory put her hands on my shoulders. "Alison," she said sharply. "Alison, I think you may be having a manic episode. There is something called manic depression and-"

"I know what manic depression is!" I shouted, stamping my feet in tantrum fashion.

Dory placed her stethoscope on my chest. "Shit, your heart is racing," she said. "Okay, Alison, here's what we're going to do. My colleague Miguel is a nurse practitioner on our mental health service." She withdrew a cordless phone from her scrub top pocket. "I'm going to call him and he'll walk you down to the emergency department-"

"No!" I cried. "I don't need that!"

Dory continued keying in numbers on the phone. "Alison," she said calmly. "Listen to yourself. You're not rational. Dr. Guerrero could have hypnotized you! You need a mental health evaluation-"

I didn't wait for her to finish. I bolted past her and miraculously made it to my car for plan B.

La Salsa sat in darkness. Even the check-cashing business was closed. Good for what I was about to do.

I walked around to the back of the restaurant where I thought the kitchen might be. A small window frame was actually loose when I tried it but wouldn't budge enough to open it. I breathed deeply for a moment and then noticed a decorative fountain with its oddly relaxing burble of water surrounded by colorful rocks. Before I knew it, I had lobbed a rock through the window. Next thing I knew I had landed on my stomach in the dark kitchen.

"Where is it?" I cried. Giant food service containers of beans and corn loomed on the shelves. With trembling hands, I took a small pen light from my purse. Was that it? A huge, unlabeled glass jar that appeared to contain several gallons of the holy-

Suddenly, the jar slipped from my perspiring hands and crashed to the floor, exploding everywhere. The police found me on my hands and knees, licking glass-impregnated salsa from the kitchen floor.

I was sentenced to and served eighteen months in prison. Dory and Joe tried their best to serve as character witnesses at my trial (Joe scratching his head absently, Dory crying), but to no avail.

I was released and had a terrible time finding a job. I will never work as a CPA again. These days, I push a broom and clean bathrooms at Fast

Burger. My new manager Trudy says I can start working the register when I gain her "trust."

Between minimum wage at Fast Burger and food stamps, I didn't starve. I finally saved up enough money to eat out. I settled on Quick Taco, the local Mexican fast food eatery. As I placed my order, I noticed a stain on my thrift shop windbreaker. When did that get there, I wondered. My mind was calculating the money I had left over for the Laundromat this week when the Quick Taco attendant produced my order of two soft tacos and an order of nachos.

"That'll be $7.73."

As I counted out the money to him, I wondered when fast food had become so expensive.

"Would you like salsa for the chips?" the attendant asked me, a boy of about seventeen with yellowed teeth encased in braces and a pimply façade.

"S—s—sure," I stuttered, watching raptly as he deposited two foil packets of salsa onto the tray.

I shuffled to a table by the window. My trembling hands addressed opening the salsa packets. I simply could not tear them open so I tore the tops with my teeth as I did many years ago as a teenager. Uncouth, but it works. As I layered the salsa on the paper tub of chips, I realized I was sobbing. I looked out the darkened window at my side, my tears mimicking the path of the raindrops on the glass.

THE GOGGLES

I tore open the FedEx box giddily. I have been fascinated by time travel since childhood and here they were – my virtual reality time travel goggles!

(Understand that I will not actually be traveling in time. Rather, the facial recognition software will allow me to see people as they looked at any time in their past or future, unless deceased. Deceased persons will only appear as shadows – soundless and faceless. The software will also allow me to see what a particular environment looked like (or will look like) at any point in time).

I paced and gleefully pumped my fists in the air as my new goggles sat on the battery charger. After what seemed an interminable period of time, they were ready to wear (or I was ready to 'travel')!

The goggles have two adjustments for traveling in time that look surprisingly old-school. One is a keypad into which you simply enter the year you want to 'travel' to. The date will always be the actual date you are wearing the goggles. The other method involves a thumbwheel in which you can either slowly or quickly move backward or forward in time. I was warned not to operate the thumbwheel too quickly because there had been media reports of people vomiting, fainting and even having psychotic episodes due to overstimulation.

I was now ready for my first "trip." I gently and slowly used the thumbwheel to go back into the past exactly one week. I was at home and sat on the couch, heart thudding in my chest as if it wanted to jump out of my ribs! There was a brief period of whiteout. Then the family room where I was sitting materialized. I was fascinated to see the carpeting in place that had since been removed in favor of laminate flooring during the past week. Cool and accurate!

I then used the keypad and typed in 2016 (four years ago). I chuckled at the minor differences I saw in the interior of our home. I hesitated when I saw a small shadow near the patio door. That was our cat who had since passed away.

I now had the courage to be more daring in my time intervals. I used the keypad to enter the year 1991. After another brief period of whiteout, I was suddenly no longer sitting on the couch in our family room. I was sitting in the middle of a corn field with a "For Sale – ¾ acre Lot" sign in view. This was entirely accurate because our home had not been built yet and was indeed not completed until 1992.

I was ready and eager to try the goggles on people at this point. My husband Bob came home and I quickly entered the year 1984 on the keypad. As he came through the door, I saw him exactly as he looked during the year we first met: deeply tanned with thick, shiny, reddish-brown hair. He was wearing the familiar red and white-striped polo shirt of his youth. I was speechless!

My next quest was to "goggle" with my 93 year-old mother. She lives in a condo in a neighboring community with live-in caregivers. I did not reveal the purpose of my visit. I knocked on the door, goggles in place, and waited. I could hear her feet shuffling in her walker in an attempt to answer the door. "Just a minute," she intoned weakly. After actually several minutes of fumbling with the door latch, she appeared – alert but frail and hunched in her walker with her wispy grey/white hair in a corona around her face.

"Hi mom," I said as I slowly adjusted the thumbwheel backwards. I was again mute as she gradually morphed from a frail, kyphotic woman of advanced age to standing with a slight hunch to regaining her exquisitely styled chestnut brown hair and porcelain complexion. But when she replied, "Hi, Susan," her voice remained aged. I learned at that moment that the goggles altered only the optics of the person using facial recognition software but not auditory characteristics such as voice. (This was a minor disappointment to me as a speech-language pathologist with a clinical interest in voice, especially vocal aging).

I came into my mother's condo and regaled my mother and her caregiver with my early experiences in using the goggles.

"Mom, what would you like to experience?" I asked.

My mother seemed reluctant, stating "This whole business scares me."

I was undeterred. I used the keypad to type in the year 1997. I suddenly found myself in another farm field because my mother's condo had not been built until 1998. I then gradually advanced the thumbwheel and experienced the thrill of slowly seeing the excavation of the basement, then beams appearing, then drywall and then all of the finishing touches as my finger slowly rotated.

I also went back to the year 1981 so that I could see my mother at the age of 55 – the age I am at this writing!

My mother started to become more curious at this point. "Can you see Tom and Dad?" she asked. My brother Tom passed away on March 14, 1984 and my dad followed him on July 20, 2007. I explained to her that the optics on the goggles only work for people currently alive. She persisted.

"Can you go back to the last time we were all together as a family?" she asked.

I stated that I was not sure regarding how the optics would process an environment that we were no longer in. Our original family home was several miles away in Hales Corners, WI and had long been under new ownership.

I sighed. "Okay, mom, I can try. Can I put the goggles on you after I make the adjustments?"

"No!" she replied, her eyes becoming anxious. "Just you try. I'm afraid."

"Afraid but curious," I chuckled as I began to adjust the goggles. Full disclosure: My brother disappeared on the evening of March 13, 1984 – a typical night in the Ides of sleet, rain and wind. He was found hanging from a tree in the park I was working in at the time on the morning of March 14, 1984. Thus, I used the keypad to enter the year 1984 and then the thumbwheel to slowly go back to the evening of March 12, 1984. I did not go to the morning or afternoon of March 13 because I had only a brief encounter with my brother that day as he slammed the door on his final exit from our home. My dad was teaching in Milwaukee on that day and I recalled my mother was not home during the day. I remembered it being my spring break from college.

My hand was sweating as I fine-tuned the thumbwheel as closely as I could to the evening of March 12, 1984 – the very last time the four of us would be together as a complete family.

There was whiteout for a long while. Then a swirling, fog-like optic appeared. My mother's youthful face and dark, generous hair smiled nervously out of the fog. I was not surprised that our family home in 1984 did not appear because we were long removed.

Then two shadows appeared – soundless and walking. The shadows joined us in a sitting position. I could see the arms moving on the shadows in a way that resembled eating. Dinner was served on the evening of March 12, 1984.

A TIME TO STOP NEEDING

I stretched out on the bed, hands clasped against the back of my cold, smooth scalp. I was thinking of how long I had been doing things. I was 55 years old, 1 month and 3 days.

Let's see: Eating solid food: (including, of course, the meal I had a few hours ago): about 54 years. Walking: also about 54 years, give or take. Speaking: around 53 years. Breathing: really for every second of those 55 years, 1 month and 3 days.

My mental inventory was interrupted by the metallic rustling of keys. The guard was having trouble opening the door again. The lock had been stubborn lately – maybe a sign of some sort. "Fuh – Jiminy Crickets!" the guard self-corrected as he struggled with the lock. I had a hard time holding back a smile observing his earnest attempt not to swear.

The door finally opened. The guard beckoned to me, his features in shadow under the bill of his cap in the dim light. "Okay, Peterson. Time to go. Get up."

I came into the hallway to join the other guards. Chaplain Joe was also there, clasping the battered leatherette bible against his chest like it was a part of his body. I had never seen him without the book during our extended time together, even though he rarely opened it. It seemed to give him something to occupy his hands, like some people toted a cigarette or a cup of coffee. "Hello, Daniel," he nodded.

We started to walk, one guard on each side and one walking very closely in back of me. We moved in step as one unit. Chaplain Joe followed off to the right side in my blind spot.

I realized how little I really knew about these men, despite the passage of time. On my left was Carl who became frustrated with small tasks like opening locks and could swear a blue streak! On my right was Marvin who was built like a linebacker and could snap chewing gum between his teeth so loudly it would echo in the corridor. (He didn't seem to be chewing tonight). In back of me, so close I could feel his body heat, was Sam. I overheard that he was going through a very nasty divorce. He seemed to lose more weight every time I saw him.

As I walked, I cocked my head toward Chaplain Joe. "Your boy play baseball tomorrow night?"

"Yep."

"Supposed to rain."

"Yeah, I heard that. They let 'em play in light rain but all bets are off if there's any lightning."

"Hmm," I replied. The chit-chat felt right and good. Almost normal!

As if reading my mind, Carl interjected. "Okay, that's enough talking, Peterson. Quiet now."

As we walked, I realized I had never been in any of these corridors despite all the years and thinking I knew my surroundings intimately.

We then arrived at a very plain metallic door. A guard I knew only vaguely stood beside it and opened it. Inside was a room with a single hospital bed in bright, almost surgical light. The only windows were in a row at the back of the room, currently obscured by curtains. A red telephone stood out starkly on one whitewashed wall.

Chaplain Joe stepped timidly into my field of vision. "May the Lord bless you, Daniel. Is there anything you need?"

I met his eyes. For the first time in decades I felt like crying. "No," I rasped. "It's time to stop needing."

My "life list" then reappeared in my mind:

Eating: done.

Walking: I estimated about 8-10 steps left.

Speaking: done.

Breathing: about 45 minutes remaining if the schedule held.

It was time to stop needing.

THE FIRST THING HE SAYS…

Stephen was hairstylist for my mother and I. We couldn't resist his classic good looks, right down to his blue-black stubble and the actual twinkle in his blue eyes. He was also a very capable hairstylist, incidentally! My mother and I always booked our appointments together. I would take the first appointment while my mother sat in the background and visited with us. She said she enjoyed watching Stephen cut my hair and transform me! A haircut that should have taken 30 minutes usually took about 75 because Stephen was acutely interested in our lives and we were in his. I suppose the social import of our visits was akin to the barbershop experience of some men. Stephen could fly from topic to topic with the ease akin to manipulating his scissors – politics, family gossip, movie reviews, cultural trends… Nothing was off limits! We could hardly wait the appointed 8 weeks between visits.

My mother and I giddily arrived for our appointment to receive our traditional group hug and kiss from Stephen. No "Me, Too Movement" standoffishness here – no sir-ree!

I sat down, already laughing as Stephen placed a cape around me. His already huge smile seemed larger than usual.

"What's going on, Stephen? You're smiling like a Cheshire cat!" I teased. I could see my mother putting on her glasses behind me in the mirror to better see the proceedings.

"Weeell," Stephen said as he sprayed my hair lightly with water. "Wouldn't you like to know..."

"Okay, cut the suspense! Let's have it!" I was never one for prolonging anything but these delightful appointments.

Stephen gently grasped a section of my hair and began to trim. "Weeell, as you know, Amy and I are newlyweds."

"Such a lucky woman," my mother intoned.

"Thanks, Gloria. So, we decided that we would still have a weekly night out with friends without one another. It keeps our relationship fresh. So my guy's night out is every Thursday."

"Go on," I said, hating the pause.

"Weeell, Dan and I had been drinking just a little bit, you know. We were walking it off and I saw the sign for lotto tickets in the Quick Mart window. On impulse, we went in for two more cans of beer and a ticket for each of us. Understand, I never play the lottery normally. I pocketed my ticket and forgot about it until I was helping Amy with the laundry two days later."

My mother could be seen in the mirror nodding and smiling approvingly.

"Sooo, I scratched off the ticket and became the instant winner of...$15,000!"

"Woo-hoo, Stephen!" we chorused. "Awesome!"

"Hey," he smiled. "At least something good came from a night of drinking."

Three hours later my mother and I were still on a post-Stephen high after lunch out. We decided to take a walk and window shop.

"I actually need a couple things from the store for dinner tonight," my mother said, gesturing toward the Hy-Vee on the other side of the street.

Twenty minutes later we exited the store – my mother with a head of lettuce and a can of chicken broth...and both of us with lottery tickets.

"Don't forget about that ticket in your purse," I quipped as my mother dropped me off at home. "I'll call you tonight," she said.

My husband Rob wasn't home yet, so I took a quick shower and sat down to look at the mail. The lottery ticket was looming large at me on the kitchen counter. I suddenly couldn't wait and raided my purse for a coin.

My legs felt weak as I found myself the instant winner of $19,200!

When I called my mother later that night, she had already long discarded her losing ticket.

Eight weeks came and went. My mother and I were giggling like kindergartners as we entered Stephen's salon for our spree of fun! After two group hugs and extra kisses, I said, "So, what up, Stephen?"

"You first!" said Mr. Dashing, eyes twinkling.

"No, YOU first."

"Okay, weeell!" Then Stephen's face split into the most capacious smile I've seen yet. "Oh, I'll just say it without preamble. Amy and I are pregnant!"

The "woo-hooing" and kissing that followed could likely be heard down the next block.

"So, life is very, very good," Stephen said as I finally climbed into the chair. "And, you may have noticed a few improvements in my salon with my lottery money!" In a sweeping gesture, he pointed out new flooring, two new mirrors and a plush rug.

More "woo-hoos" and hugs followed the disclosure of my lottery win.

"Stephen, you are my good luck charm," I teased.

Stephen blushed modestly in response.

"You are going to have a beautiful child," my mother said in the mirror.

"Anything would be an improvement on this mug," Stephen retorted as we groaned.

On the way home, my mother reached over and touched my hand. "I'm so happy for Stephen," she said, eyes still on the road. "He'll make a wonderful father."

"I know," I said, suddenly surprised at the choked quality in my voice.

"Oh, honey. Your time will come." My mother knew that Rob and I had been trying to get pregnant for almost a year.

"All in due time, I suppose," I replied.

"There IS a time for everything," my mother reassured.

Two firsts happened almost 8 weeks later: (1) I almost canceled my part of the appointment with Stephen because I wasn't feeling well. My mother talked me into going, manipulative woman that she is! (2) I found out I was pregnant!!

Stephen's salon is about 40 miles away. Yes, we drive to another county to see him. I would actually drive to the ends of the earth to keep Stephen as my hairstylist. He also appeared to be my good luck charm because the first thing he always said happened to me, too!

The usual giddiness was at a whole new level. I even thought of not letting Stephen go first with his news update so I could blurt out the joy of my upcoming maternity. But when we came into the salon the lights were off and Stephen was sitting with his back to us. Was he asleep? Was he not expecting us? Impossible!

"Stephen! Hey!" We converged on him.

His movements in standing up were stiff and effortful, like those of an old man. His skin was sallow and dark shadows ran beneath his eyes. His clothing appeared one size too big and his shirt was actually buttoned incorrectly.

"Stephen?" My mother and I gently touched his shoulder. He seemed frail enough to fall.

Finally, Stephen cleared his throat. He did not meet our eyes. A dry, papery voice emanated from him with a slight tremor.

"Uh...appointment's still on for today but then I'll be closing up for a while. Maybe a long while." He swallowed. "It's Amy. She was in a car accident on the expressway about ten days ago. She's in a coma. A deep one. Minimal brain function. So I have some decisions to make."

My car keys, still clutched tightly in my perspiring hand, clattered involuntarily to the floor.

Stephen was hairstylist for my mother and I. We couldn't resist his classic good looks, right down to his blue-black beard stubble and the actual twinkle...

AWAY

"It'll just be snacks and drinks and a tour of the new house," my husband reassured me as we pulled into the circle drive of his boss's home. My husband Jim had recently been promoted at the small advertising agency and this get-together appeared to be part housewarming and part post-promotion congratulation.

"Gil's wife is a runner," Jim remarked as we unbuckled our seat belts. I reached into the back seat for the small decorative palm that constituted our housewarming gift.

"Oh, really? Marathoning?"

"No, I think shorter distance stuff. Oh, and Gil was a tennis champion in college."

"So these people are jocks!" I quipped as Jim rang the doorbell.

Gil answered the door. He was slim in his white Hilfiger polo and tan cargo shorts. A neatly trimmed goatee graced his dimpled chin.

"Jim!" Gil roared warmly. "You didn't tell me your wife was this fantastically gorgeous!"

"She defies earthly description in her loveliness!" Jim retorted. "Gil, this is my wife Sandra."

"So, so pleased to meet you!" Gil returned. "And this is my wife Deborah."

Deborah extended her hand to me. She definitely had the compact runner's build in her cream-colored Capri pants and a mauve summer sweater. "Nice to meet you," she said in a quiet, earnest tone as her chestnut brown hair bounced slightly at her ears.

"Well, come on in," said Gil. "You guys are our first official visitors since the rest of the family is out of state."

We entered a great room with a fieldstone fireplace and a skylight that showered rays of sunlight onto plush oriental rugs. A kitchen big enough for a commercial operation beckoned with stainless steel appliances to one side and a home office to the other.

"We thought we'd give you a tour and then have some snacks. Deborah's homemade Crab Rangoon is a delight. How about a drink?" Gil looked at us with anticipation. "I just opened some cabernet or there's beer in the fridge. I could also mix you something. I got a great bottle of Scotch for Christmas last year that's never been opened."

"I'll take some of the cab, as long as it's open," I said.

"A beer, please," Jim said, predictably.

I presented the palm to Deborah who said she had "just the spot for it." As I sipped my wine, I studied a family portrait opposite the fireplace – Gil, Deborah and a blond-haired, cherubic-looking toddler that must have been their daughter.

Jim and Gil had already departed on a tour of the upstairs level.

Deborah sidled up to me, also sipping some cab. I was about to ask how old their daughter was when she said," You know, this fireplace is a feat of engineering. I took photos of the construction. You should see some of these stones prior to the installation – boulders, really. Here, let me show you."

She led me to a huge leather sectional and we pondered construction photos of the fireplace and then other aspects of the home being built.

By that time, Jim and Gil had returned downstairs from the remainder of the tour. Maybe it was my imagination but Jim looked pale to me. Hmm. Maybe nerves in visiting the boss at home. He had been working extremely hard lately… As if reading my mind, Jim smiled at me reassuringly.

"Gil, is that your tennis trophy case?" Jim interjected.

Gil ushered him to a massive glass curio case loaded with various trophies, most adorned with sculpted figures smashing a tennis ball. "Yes, I'm afraid that's all in the past. I played in college and I was definitely good enough to go pro. But then I met Deborah and I couldn't face living out of suitcases and airports. Being an ad man, I can be home for dinner. My wife and 5 year-old daughter are really everything to me."

Deborah stood up, returning the photo album to the coffee table. "Sandra, how about a tour? More cab?"

"Yes to your first question, no thank you to your second," I replied.

As Gil and Jim laughed raucously about something, we ascended the stairs.

"The master has a gorgeous view of the marsh," Deborah said as we walked to the window. "Our backyard is a wetland conservancy so it'll never get developed."

"The privacy will be nice," I added.

"This is a storage closet – very spacious," Deborah gestured to the door. "You can never have enough storage space."

"True," I said.

Suddenly I heard a soft grunting sound – almost like a muffled "Hmmf."

"What was that?" I said reflexively. I gripped my wine glass, startled.

"Oh, Gil piled all of his tennis stuff in there. That's why the door is closed. It's a mess in there. It's probably something shifting in there."

"No, I don't think-" I began.

I was further startled when Deborah clapped her hands sharply together. "Shall we continue the tour?"

She then showed me her daughter's room. "This is Gabriella's room," she said. The room was a sea of pink lace, suitable for a fairy princess. The characters from "Frozen" heavily influenced the décor.

"How old is your daughter?" I asked.

"She'll already be six in two weeks. They grow so fast!"

"She loves "Frozen," doesn't she?"

Deborah smiled with a tinge of what might have been sadness. "Yeah, they all love "Frozen" at that age…"

"Will Gabriella be joining us today?"

"No, she's staying with her grandmother in Ithaca. But she'll be home in plenty of time for her birthday."

The rest of the afternoon continued with polite servings of finger foods, including the storied Crab Rangoon.

"Guys, how about staying for supper? It's no trouble. I can throw a couple steaks on the grill," Gil said, leaning forward in his chair and rolling an empty beer bottle idly in his hands.

I was grateful when Jim interjected with "We'll take a rain check. But thank you for your hospitality. We had a wonderful time and we hope to return the favor soon."

As we pulled back onto the highway, silence prevailed for about a mile. I broke it.

"Jim, something is wrong."

"What? Are you okay, honey?"

"No, not me. Back at Gil and Deborah's. Deborah was giving me the upstairs tour and I heard a weird sound like a grunt coming from the hallway closet."

Without a word, Jim gently pulled the car over to the shoulder.

"Do they have a dog that they were keeping confined during our visit?" I asked.

"No," Jim practically scoffed. "Gil's allergic." He shifted uncomfortably in his seat and detached the seat belt. He rubbed his palms on his thighs and met my eyes. "I heard the sound, too," he almost whispered. "Gil didn't react at all but quickly moved me along for another beer."

"And what about their daughter? Deborah said she was staying with her grandmother in Ithaca."

The color drained from Jim's face. "When we were upstairs, Gil told me that Gabriella was away at summer camp."

"Not even close!" I exclaimed. "Jim, we have to do something. Something's not right here."

Jim looked at me levelly and calmly but his voice assumed a pleading tone: "Sandra, we're talking about my boss here. If we're wrong..."

"Jim, a child could be in danger!" I almost shrieked.

"Okay, okay, okay." Jim was perspiring on his upper lip now. He shifted in his seat and withdrew his wallet from his back pocket. He took out a quarter. "All right, Sandra. Heads, we call the police. Tails, we mind our own business."

I held my breath as the coin flipped, falling onto the floormat between Jim's feet. He then slowly looked up at me and resolutely nodded his head.

INTERIOR

Interior. The weather-beaten sign announcing this desolate South Dakota town just outside of the Badlands caught my attention through my bug-spattered windshield. Heat shimmered off the road – the dry, windy type of heat that is typical of August in South Dakota. I was fleeing a nasty unilateral divorce when I left Belvidere, Illinois three days ago. I knew I was going west but not specifically where. Seattle? Los Angeles? Ditch the car for a plane ticket to Hawaii? I only knew that I wanted to go far. Maybe Interior was far enough.

The trailer was on a dusty, unpaved road being sold by the owner, a wizened Lakota woman. She affectionately called it a "ranch" and took cash for the entire purchase. Everything from my life in Belvidere was in the back seat of my Subaru or in the trunk. I was home.

Three weeks later, I had settled into the predictable routine of a hermit. I spent a large part of my days in the battered lawn chair in back of my newly acquired "ranch," looking at the timeless rock formations of the Badlands until they grew almost inky purple in the ever- earlier gathering dusk. My cell phone remained charged but silent.

I cooked simple meals on the ancient cook stove in the trailer and drew water from a faucet that vibrated and shook as it coursed through. I talked to no one. On a walk, I discovered a family about one mile up the road on a small farm with two horses. On subsequent walks, I noticed a man in about his thirties tending to the two horses and sometimes to two school-aged children – an active boy and a slightly more reclusive girl. An older woman who could have been their grandmother stood austerely looking out from the porch of the farmhouse, hand shielding her eyes from the gauzy early September sunlight. I think she saw me on the road.

I continued to walk and maintain a silent life every day. The Subaru stood forgotten, key still in the ignition.

On a mid-September morning, I awoke and stiffly stumble-walked to the tiny kitchen, automatically filling my tea kettle from the ever-shaky faucet. I flipped the light switch and nothing happened. Puzzled, I tried the ancient kitschy lamp that the Lakota woman had left behind on the kitchen table. Nothing.

I continued with the TV, although it only received three channels quite badly. It too remained dark.

I lifted the blinds in the small sitting area to reveal sky of a robin's egg blue with filtered, late summer sunlight. A storm was clearly not to blame, although the lights had flickered three nights ago as rain battered the humble roof of the trailer.

I then thought of the camping equipment still in the trunk of the Subaru. I had planned on alternating hotel stays with camping to save money in my wandering. I retrieved a battery-powered lantern and a small propane camp stove from the car.

I then thought of the radio – a multi-band deal with a dedicated weather band. Most of my "radio" listening was via podcasts or streaming stations on the Internet, but this radio was my late father's prized possession. I smiled as I thought of him driving me to soccer practice with an AM radio station crackling through the speakers.

I checked my cell phone first. It was completely dead and of course could not be charged without electricity.

Then I sat in the battered lawn chair with the radio, carefully pulling out and angling the antenna to facilitate reception as my father had taught me. Bursts of static alternating with silence were all I could find even with careful fine-tuning. The enormity of the outage then began to vaguely alarm me.

After tea heated on the camp stove, I decided to take a walk. It was getting hot in the trailer without any trees to shade it in the noonday sun. I walked in the same direction as always, coming upon the small farm. The children and older woman were not evident but the man was in front of the house, chopping wood in a hideously stained t-shirt. I hesitated, feeling the dirt scuffling under my feet. I wanted to talk to him, but I realized I hadn't spoken to anyone since the Lakota woman sold me the trailer. I cleared my throat and walked toward him across the scruffy yard.

The man did not seem to notice me as his eyes and arms continued intent on his work.

My voice sounded slow and hollow when I said, "Hi!" about eight feet from him.

The man lowered the ax gently in mid-swing and let it fall to the ground. He wiped the sweat from his eyes and then shaded them with a work-worn hand.

"Help you?" he said.

"Hi," I said redundantly. "I'm Blair. I live about a mile-" I stopped talking to gesture in the direction of the trailer.

The man stood stock still, hand still shading his eyes. "Yeah. I see you walking."

I shifted nervously from foot to foot.

"I'm Ed," he added.

Grateful for something resembling potential civility, I quickly said, "Your power out, too?"

"Yuh."

"Oh. Does it happen often here?"

"N'really. Maybe in a t-storm for a coupla hours, but no, nothing like this." Ed seemed unconcerned.

"Your cell phone work?" I asked.

"Don't have one."

"Oh. Landline?"

"Dead as a doornail," Ed said flatly. "Like everything else."

"Are you…concerned?"

"No, but my kids are. They're driving me crazy because they can't play on the X-Box. Chores aren't their thing, as you can see," said Ed, gesturing expansively to the solitude around him. "We have a wood-burning stove. That's why I'm getting busy with the woodpile. My mom's fixing lunch."

"Okay…." I was at a loss. "Well…I guess we'll stay in touch. Have you seen any trucks from the power company?"

"Nope."

"Okay, Ed, well, see you around." He said nothing in reply and I turned on my heel and left.

After another week of camp stove meals, solitude and no electricity, I decided to drive into town for provisions. I became a compulsive checker of the radio for any outside communication, but to no avail. Not even the storied "Emergency Broadcast System."

With three cans of soup left in my kitchen inventory, I ventured into the Subaru. It smelled vaguely of must and disuse. The key still dangled in the ignition. I reflexively turned it over with no results. To use Ed's words, "Dead as a doornail." I cursed myself for not using the car since handing cash to the wizened Lakota woman.

I sat briefly on the front steps of the trailer, weighing my options. It was roughly three miles to the Hy-Vee grocery store in town. I could walk and load a backpack, but that wouldn't be much volume of food…

I closed my eyes and raised my face to the sun. I dozed on those steps but something prevented me from a full sleep. It was the clip-clop of multiple horse hooves on the dusty road.

When I opened my eyes, it was Ed – visibly thinner and still in the hideously stained t-shirt, albeit with an equally hideous lime green warm-up jacket over it.

Ed was on horseback. Lashed to his horse was a riderless horse. I saw Ed's eyes clocking to the open door of the Subaru, keys still dangling in the ignition.

He shaded his eyes in his trademark way. "Morning," he said.

"Morning. Ed, right?"

"Yup. Blair?"

"Good memory."

The breeze riffled as the conversation stalled.

"Okay," Ed finally said. "Come on."

"What?"

"Grocery shopping time. Here's your ride. Her name is Ginger."

On the way to town, we talked of continued lack of electricity and the failure of seemingly all motor vehicles and heavy equipment.

"It's EMP, we think," Ed said stoically. "Maybe a terrorist attack. Maybe a nuclear attack."

"But I don't see wreckage," I countered, patting Ginger reassuringly. "I didn't hear or see anything."

Ed looked up to the sky as if the answer might bloom there. He remained silent.

Town was a...SHOCK. Cars cluttered the proximal stretches of highway, clearly long abandoned. One Jeep had "HELP ME" lettered on the dusty hood. Ed and I navigated the horses between a mish-mash of stalled cars in front of the Hy-Vee store. He pointed to a light post at the far end of the cluttered parking lot. "I'll tie up the horses there," he said, a startled expression on his careworn face.

I dismounted Ginger somewhat clumsily, given that I hadn't been on a horse since summer camp as a ten year-old! Ed swiftly tied the horses to the light post and then proffered me a large, battered canvas bag.

"Here!" he said. "Go and get whatever you can. We'll divide it up later."

I was taken aback. I was a bit afraid to go into the grocery store given the panicked, uncivilized-looking crowds going in and out.

Ed read my facial expression. "Look, you have got to go in there. I have to stay with the horses or someone will steal them." He patted Ginger's flank. "These guys are valuable transportation these days. Or I could go in and you can guard the horses. But be prepared to fight." He then folded back his warm-up jacket to reveal a gun tucked in his waistband. "I didn't bring you along just for the company."

I swallowed hard and turned around. My heart was pounding so hard my vision seemed to jump. "It's just grocery shopping," I murmured to myself. "Calm down."

A rabble of fatigued-looking and many unkempt people were spilling in and out of the store. I was jostled so many times on the way in that I almost lost my balance. It was as if no one saw me.

The store was very dark despite the daylight. No overhead music played so the pounding of feet, the slamming of boxes and the occasional shout were the only soundtrack. The air was warm, stuffy and fetid.

I hugged the worn canvas bag to my chest as I ventured into the produce area. Nothing was left except for a single rotten banana and two tomatoes smashed on the floor.

The butcher/meat case was completely bare. A disheveled-looking employee stood staring out behind the counter, motionless. The smell was rancid despite the absence of products.

I then felt an urgency to find SOMETHING! The canned food aisles were completely empty; however, at the far end of one, I noticed a knot of about three people grabbing simultaneously for something on the shelf.

I may have to fight after all, I thought.

My courage returned. I approached the people. I could see that two of them were fighting over a container of Spam. The third person was reaching between the legs of the other two to reach for a can of chili that had fallen onto the floor. All were oblivious to my approach.

Suddenly, the can of Spam slipped from the hands of the two raging customers. I watched as if in slow motion as the can made a small arc up into the air. Then the can hit the ground and scuttled like a hockey puck, coming to rest at my feet. I quickly grabbed the can and flung it into the canvas bag to the cry of "Bitch!" from one of the customers. I turned and began to run as their anger was palpable. The tiny bit of weight in the canvas bag felt good, even if it was a food I detested in ordinary times.

I came upon a small section of outdoor goods, including matches, chemical fire logs, lighter fluid and the like. A dazed-looking woman grabbed for the last box of matches just as I did. We looked at each other in silence for a moment. Would I have to pry it from her fingers, I wondered. Then the woman sighed and whispered something that sounded like "uncle" and slunk away.

I felt momentary guilt wielding the wrinkled packaging around the matches but I had heard about the enormity of a South Dakota winter.

I left the store twenty minutes later with my life, a can of Spam, a pouch of prunes and other dehydrated fruit, two bottled waters, a dented can of lighter fluid and two boxes of Grape Nuts cereal. I was ready to pay but the cash registers were of course not operational and the only front-of-store employee was sitting dejectedly behind the glass at the service counter as people stormed in and out. Ed was ready with the horses.

Over the next four months, I learned much about the good and bad sides of human nature.

At Hy-Vee (our one and only trip there), I saw animalistic greed.

But I also saw so much good as winter raged around us.

I saw Ed's compassion when he came on Ginger on that cold early December morning to get me, finding me nearly frozen under a pile of dirty blankets in the trailer.

I gained a family over the next few weeks as Ed welcomed me into his home. His children, Jack and Lily, were lovely despite the X-Box deprivation.

I gained a warm and and practical friend in Ed's mother, Carmine. She kept my fear away by keeping me busy – simple strategy, but effective. I learned that Carmine had moved in with Ed and the children after Ed's wife had an affair with a co-worker.

I learned patience from Ed. I learned fortitude from him as well, this man who could hunt tirelessly for twelve hours so we could have a paltry amount of meat. I learned that he was a pediatric cardiologist in Minneapolis before escaping to Interior.

I learned generosity without fanfare from Carmine. I learned that she gave us larger food portions than she gave herself and often ate in the kitchen instead of with us in the dining room, stating that she was preparing something so we wouldn't notice she was starving herself.

I learned even deeper sadness when Carmine died on a Sunday with an outside temperature of minus 20.

The power never came back on.

MERCY

It was just past dawn at Victor's Diner, a small greasy spoon in the middle of the New Mexico desert. We were gathered in Victor's cramped back office. Victor was the owner, manager and sole cook. I had been a waitress there for the past thirteen years (Victor preferred the term "server"), my longest stint in the profession yet.

Victor sat at the battered desk that dominated the small, dark room with World War II era green linoleum. His feet were crossed carelessly on top of the cluttered desk. You can feel free to do that when you're the boss.

"Lenore, meet Valerie," Victor gestured with a smile to the young woman standing in back of me. "She's our new server."

I turned around to behold Valerie. She smiled shyly at me. She appeared to be about twenty years old with a petite build and wispy light brown curls that she nervously pushed away from her eyes.

"Well, it's about time!" I crowed. "We've been short for so long, I wondered if we'd ever get another waitress."

"Server," Victor quickly corrected.

Victor's Diner was definitely a "skeleton" operation in terms of staffing. Historically, we had only two waitresses (oops – servers) and we were open 7 AM to 7 PM seven days a week. Our clientele was mostly truckers and travelers. There were really no neighborhood regulars given our remote location. I personally liked the anonymous clientele. Despite being a waitress, I was not one for chit-chat.

Victor consulted his watch and stood up, straightening his apron. "Okay, time for me to start slinging eggs. Lenore, please welcome Valerie."

Instead, I retorted, "Isn't she a little 'wet behind the ears'?"

Valerie looked completely puzzled as she pushed another strand of curl away from her eyes.

"I mean, Victor, you hire 'em so young and then they aren't reliable," I said bitterly. I had worked many a solo Saturday or Sunday because the other server was up to no good the night before.

Victor smiled warmly at both of us. "I have confidence in Valerie and in you, too, Lenore." He then brushed past us to open the kitchen.

I briefly regarded Valerie. She appeared to be a poster child for callow youth and inexperience. "Okay, you can start by rolling up silverware into napkins. Once the rush hits, everyone is crying for an extra spoon or fork. Go on," I directed her.

"What do you mean by silverware?" Valerie's voice was as tiny and timid as she was.

I froze. Was this a joke of some kind? Was she special needs? That would be just like Victor to hire someone like that, good and noble Victor!

"Seriously?" I hissed but I hadn't time to berate her. In ten minutes, the small, dusty parking lot would be filling up. "C'mon, I'll show you." We walked into the seating area.

Breakfast service actually went better than expected, once Valerie learned what silverware was. She was actually a very quick observational learner, which was handy because every stool and booth were filled. It seemed she never stopped watching me but she also made no major mistakes without a direct training session.

At mid-morning, business predictably slowed. I was dunking a tea bag into hot water for myself at the counter. We were down to one customer in a booth in Valerie's zone. Valerie approached me clasping the menu.

"Excuse me," she opened.

"Yeah?"

"Ah...What are scrambled eggs?" she whispered. "The customer wants two of them."

I groaned. "You are killing me, kid! Where are you from that you never heard of scrambled eggs?"

Valerie's young forehead crinkled slightly and her lips pursed into a frown. "I know the type of egg where it's like a large white area on the bottom with a small, round yellow area in the middle," she offered.

I couldn't help but laugh. "Give the girl a gold star!" I bellowed as her customer looked up at me somewhat uncomfortably. I shifted gears. "You go back to the kitchen and ask ol' Victor what scrambled eggs are." I had no compunction about setting a trap and Valerie took the bait, menu in hand. I then did her the favor of warming her customer's coffee.

Five minutes went by, then ten. It was very quiet throughout the diner. The customer was scrolling through his phone, patiently awaiting two scrambled eggs. I decided to check on Victor and Valerie. As I walked back to the kitchen, I wondered if he fired her on the spot.

I could see both of them through the short order service window. They were standing with their backs turned away from me at the griddle.

"My mother used to add milk to her scrambled eggs to increase fluffiness, but I'm more of a butter guy," Victor said in a tender, fatherly tone as he brandished a stick of butter. Valerie watched intently and nodded her head. Victor carefully plated the eggs and smiled warmly at Valerie. "And there you have it – scrambled eggs, Victor-style!" He bowed comically and she laughed.

"Hey, hungry customer out here!" I called through the service window.

Victor handed me the plate.

"Oh, now I get to serve HER customer?" I wailed sarcastically.

After serving the eggs and providing one more warm-up to the customer's coffee, I stormed back to the kitchen. Victor was hunched over the griddle, vigorously cleaning in anticipation of the lunch crowd.

"What's the deal with her, Vic?" I fumed.

Victor stopped scrubbing for a moment. "She takes an interest in different parts of the business, not just serving."

"You mean waitressing."

Victor looked at me kindly. "So how did she do this morning, Lenore?"

I bit my lip hard, managing to zip out "Fine!"

"Well, okay then!" Victor said expansively. "That's all I want!" He went back to scrubbing a stubborn stain on the griddle.

"Vic, she didn't even know what silverware or scrambled eggs are!"

"She does now!"

"You're missing the point. Don't you think this is a little weird, Vic?"

He stopped scrubbing and looked up at Lenore with a plaintive expression. "Words, Lenore. They're just words," he almost whispered. "Now you've got to let me go. Lunch is upon us!"

The next week passed surprisingly smoothly until the customer's request for the baseball game.

Valerie was pouring coffee for a customer seated at the counter when he asked her to turn the TV on and find the baseball game. I could see Valerie freeze and panic out of my peripheral vision as I was putting some glasses away.

"Baseball?" she asked in clear confusion.

The customer wiped his lips with a napkin. "Just turn the TV on and flip through the channels. I'll tell you when you've got the game, okay?"

Valerie smiled and nodded pertly. I made no move to assist her. I confess to being a bit puzzled when she climbed up on a stepstool to address the darkened TV. The customer and I watched as she felt around the set to discern how to power it on. The remote control happened to be in my uniform pocket. I couldn't help but giggle. The customer scoffed and said, "Aw, just forget it, lady."

Suddenly, Victor appeared out of nowhere. He squinted at Valerie on the stepstool and glared at the customer.

"Give me the remote, Lenore," Victor said flatly as he helped Valerie down to the floor. I will never know how he decided I had possession of it!

Victor took the remote control and slapped it on the counter. He turned to the snickering customer. "Get out," he said calmly. "You are not welcome here." Then, he turned to me. "I'm suspending you for the rest of the day, Lenore. No pay. You will treat your co-worker with respect."

My jaw dropped involuntarily as Victor proceeded to show Valerie how to use the TV remote.

I slept very little that night. This job was not a flash in the pan for me. I had "roots" at the diner after thirteen years of waitressing (oops – serving) there. I didn't want to spoil my relationship with Victor but I had so many unanswered questions about Valerie and her apparent ignorance of basic things. So I pulled into the parking lot at 6:30 AM. Victor's car was already there so I anticipated a few minutes to speak earnestly with him before the diner opened.

Victor was in the back office, half-glasses perched on his nose, opening up the mail. He straightened in his chair when he saw me.

"Lenore."

"Victor."

"Sit." I did.

Victor leaned back in his swivel chair with a creaking noise. "Lenore, I never thought of you as a bully, but yesterday…"

"It's just…" I tried not to sound overly anxious but I couldn't. "Victor, what's her deal? Is she mentally challenged?"

"No."

"She's not a foreigner, is she? Maybe that would explain some of it."

"No."

"Well, Victor, don't you think all of this is more than a little strange?"

Victor leaned back so far that the swivel chair was now touching the wall. He clasped both hands on top of his head, apparently very deep in thought.

"Where is she from?" I demanded.

"Why don't you ask her yourself?"

"Victor, where did she come from?" I persisted.

Victor sighed and lumbered over to the ancient green file cabinet that held the life of the business, including the scant personnel records. He pulled out a manila file folder and rummaged through it. He looked at me earnestly over the top of his half-glasses. "New York," he said.

"New York City?"

"That's what I have."

"So how does someone from New York City not know silverware or scrambled eggs or how to turn on a TV?"

Victor shrugged. "Is she doing a good job out there?"

I was so frustrated I felt tears coming. "Yes," I sputtered.

We closed thirty minutes early on the evening of Victor's 58th birthday. He had a surprise for us. He had been baking all afternoon. Valerie and I were seated at the counter as he carefully brought in a gigantic double chocolate cake. We clapped as he gracefully placed it on the counter.

"Now I would like to treat my two favorite servers to my great grandmother's double chocolate cake!"

The obligatory rounds of out-of-tune "Happy Birthday" followed. (Valerie clearly didn't know the song, but I had stopped questioning anything at this point).

Victor then served our slices. I plunged right in. "Ooh, heavenly, Victor!" I said in garbled speech, my mouth brimming with chocolate.

Valerie smiled warmly at both of us but her slice of cake sat untouched.

"Go on, try it!" I crowed, licking my fingers.

She shook her head. "I can't," she whispered.

"Well, why not? It's the best!" I chortled.

Victor was wiping his hands and regarding Valerie with that fatherly concern but remained silent.

"Why not?" I pushed.

Valerie shook her head dejectedly.

"Are you on a diet or something?" I persisted. Victor glared at me. Oops, my sensitivity chip was malfunctioning again. Did she have an eating disorder? In fact, I didn't recall ever seeing her eat or drink on the job! Wait, I also didn't remember her ever using the restroom either, now that I thought about it!

"I'm sorry," Valerie said in a querulous voice. "Sorry to disappoint you." Then she left the diner.

Victor gently put a hand on my arm. "Don't follow her. Just let it go," he murmured.

Victor left to continue his birthday celebration with his wife and family. I stayed a bit later to mop the floor. I left in full darkness just before

9:00. The night wind had a slight chill and I pulled my sweater tightly around me as I reached into my purse for my car key fob.

It was then that I noticed her car.

Valerie was still here, sitting in her car in the parking lot. It was just she and I for miles around. I became concerned, wondering if she was having car trouble. But why wouldn't she have come back into the diner if that was the case? I decided to check on her, feeling Victor's approval as I approached her car.

Valerie was in the driver's seat. She had what looked like a neon orange flute between her lips. Was it a musical instrument? Suddenly, her cheeks flared and she drained the flute, swallowing the contents. Then, much to my horror, her skin and eyes turned the same neon orange!

I dropped my purse and ran. By then, Valerie had seen me. "Wait, Lenore!" she called in her sweet, earnest tone. "Don't be scared! This is just how we – I – eat! The color goes away after a while, see?"

But I didn't see because I was peeling out of the parking lot, kicking up desert dust and gravel into the neon orange haze.

The night of my recent suspension was restful compared to the night of Valerie's "reveal."

I arrived for work in the pre-dawn. Victor's car was there and a car I didn't recognize. Valerie's car was not in evidence. I was shaking as I headed toward the back office, unsure of what I would tell Victor.

Victor sat at his desk, apparently doing nothing. His hands were clasped gently across his chest.

"Sit," he said.

I did.

Victor cleared his throat. "Valerie resigned last night. She actually called me at home."

I was silent.

"Lenore, I treat people well no matter who they are or where they're from. That's how I roll. I expect you to do the same."

I nodded stiffly.

"Lenore, meet Susan, the new server." I turned around to regard her.

Victor continued. "I'm giving you one more chance, Lenore. But if you ever treat Susan with any disrespect, I will immediately terminate your employment."

I swallowed and continued looking at Susan. She held my gaze and raised her chin slightly as Victor admonished me.

"Okay, then." Victor was on his feet now. "We have breakfast to serve."

THE NOTE WRITER

The funeral director handed me her card in the dim twilight. "I'll see you tomorrow morning," she said softly. "Call us if you need anything at all. We will take good care of your mom."

I nodded and placed the card in my purse. I stood at the front door as the funeral director wheeled my mother's body down the sidewalk toward a black SUV. Then I turned out the lights and sat in the dark.

My mother passed away at home after a bout of bacterial pneumonia further complicated by a stroke. I felt lucky to be able to assist in her care during those final days, even though she was essentially mute. We had always been close – no "terrible teenage years" or other rifts between us.

I arrived at the funeral home to make her final arrangements promptly at 9 AM, as arranged the night before. A young woman smiled wanly at me as she opened the massive oak front door.

"May I help you?" Her voice was almost completely absorbed by the quietude of our surroundings.

"Yes, I have an appointment to plan my mother's funeral."

"Do you remember who you are meeting with?"

I opened my purse to retrieve the business card. I pulled the card out, noticing that a purple post-it note was now attached to it. Funny. I didn't remember that being there and neither my mother nor I used post-it notes. I peeled off the post-it note to reveal the funeral director's name. "Mandy," I told the young woman.

"Thank you. It'll be just one moment. Please have a seat. Would you like water or coffee?"

"No thank you."

The young woman left.

I sat down in the extreme quiet and turned over the purple post-it note. My heart slammed in my chest as I saw my mother's distinctive, picture-perfect, Palmer method cursive relaying the following message:

> DON'T WORRY ABOUT ME, HONEY.
> EVERYTHING IS GOING TO BE FINE.
> LOVE,
> MAMA

I could barely swallow. My heart seemed to rise in my chest. When had she written that note? The post-it note itself appeared crisp and new, not dog-eared or soiled.

My mother had always been a note writer. Her brief missives were usually well-timed messages of hope and encouragement when I needed it most. My mind went back to my middle school years. At this point, my mother was still placing a note in my lunch box almost every day. I was now in the sixth grade. I was eating lunch with a new friend, Danielle Borkovec and her posse. I took out my sandwich wrapped in my mother's signature wax paper. At the same time, a note from my mother tumbled out onto the table.

"What's that?" said Danielle through a huge bite of her burger. Danielle truly wolfed her food despite her petite figure.

"Nothing," I said, quickly putting the note back into my lunch box.

"It's not nothing!" Danielle persisted.

Before I knew it, Danielle had spun my lunch box around and snatched it.

"Hey!" I shot back, feeling violated.

As Danielle's posse gathered closer beside her, she retrieved my mother's note from my lunch box and proceeded to read it aloud in a strident, sarcastic tone: "Just remember I think of you and miss you during the day! You'll always be my little girl. Love, Mama."

I could feel my cheeks burning with shame. I willed myself not to cry.

Danielle clasped the note to her chest with mock sincerity. "Aw, mama's little girl!" she shrieked.

As I looked around, everyone was laughing for at least three tables on either side of us.

And so began a period of isolation in my twelve year-old life. No more lunches with Danielle or her posse. I dreaded seeing them in the school corridors. The proceedings would invariably go something like this:

DANIELLE: "Aw, look! It's mama's little girl!"

ME: (nothing/ silence)

By the end of the school year, I was known as "MLG."

Oddly, after the initial hurt and embarrassment wore off, I found that I didn't mind the moniker. Danielle and her minions obviously did not have mothers who cared for them as deeply as my mother cared for me. By the time school ended for the summer, I had transitioned from pitying myself to pitying them.

Three weeks after my mother's funeral, I returned to my position as a legal secretary in a small patent law firm. The firm was indeed small – just myself and Jeremy T. Grandbeck , Attorney-at-Law. Jeremy quietly welcomed me back in his kind , grandfatherly fashion.

At mid-morning, I was busily keyboarding a brief when Jeremy arrived in my office accompanied by a young man. He appeared to be about 30 years old and wore a shiny navy blue suit with a candy red bowtie. His dark wavy hair was slicked back and he wore narrow rectangular-shaped glasses.

"Carolyn, meet Alfred Polacheck," intoned Jeremy in his sleepy bass voice. "Alfred will be joining the firm as an associate patent attorney. I believe it's time to expand our staff. As you know, I'm not getting any younger."

Alfred leaned forward to politely shake my proffered hand.

"Now, then," continued Jeremy in his typical patrician tone. "I will leave him with you for a tour and orientation to the office. If you will excuse me."

After Jeremy left, I invited Alfred to sit down. I closed the door of my office and regarded him.

Alfred was conspicuously yawning, so much so that his eyes were watering. He appeared to be on the verge of sleep.

I started to laugh –first lightly, then raucously. I knew I was taking a chance here, given that Alfred and I hadn't even spoken yet. "You're feeling it, too, aren't you?" I gasped between laughs.

Alfred rolled his eyes and began barking with laughter. "That dude is so boring! I was afraid my head was going to hit his desk when he was talking to me! It was all I could do not to fall into a coma!"

I was wiping my streaming eyes. This was the hardest I'd laughed in many months. While a kind and fair boss, Jeremy was indeed a Class A Bore. I remembered a staff meeting (i.e. just Jeremy and myself) during which I nodded off. When I jerked awake, Jeremy was still droning on but (lucky for me) he had broken eye contact to scroll through something on his computer. Whew –close one!

"By the way, you can call me Al." Al was barely intelligible through his breathless laughter.

I smiled back. This was going to be fun!

On Thursday, I was preparing a past-due invoice when I saw Al enter my office in my peripheral vision. I was under the gun to get this invoice done *so it could go into the mail today. Jeremy had been adamant. Thus, I did not look up from my work as Al came in.*

"Excuse me."

"Yes, Al. Busy here. What do you need?"

I could see him angling himself in various ways to try to get me to look at him.

"Dude, where is the water cooler?" Al asked.

"You know where," I shot back, still not looking up.

Al was apparently not going to leave.

My eyes stayed locked on my desktop computer screen. "Your glasses are on upside-down again. Dude, you need a new joke. This is the third time this week!" My will then caved and I finally capitulated, looking at Al and his lame upside-down glasses.

I continued. "Dude, is this pre-school or a prestigious patent law firm?"

Al quickly stuck out his tongue at me and left.

I will admit that Al became a guilty pleasure at work, this man-child, this clown-attorney. I stopped in his office to deliver a ream of printer paper.

"Come on in, dude," he said, leaning back in his chair. No bow tie today, just a crisp, baby blue, open-collared shirt with a cream-colored suit.

I nodded at him and placed the box of printer paper on top of a filing cabinet. I then walked over to the opposite wall to inspect his framed law degree.

"Whatcha doin' there, Carolyn-dude?"

"I'm just making sure that you're really an attorney, because you're such a slackerish goofball!" I retorted as we descended into another giggling fit.

One day about three weeks later, Al walked into my office with his arms clasped behind his back.

"Dude," I greeted.

"Dude."

"Wassup?"

Al stood in front of me, hands still concealed behind his back. "Left hand or right hand? Pick one."

"Left hand."

He deposited a package of chocolate cupcakes on my desk. "Oh, man. That means I get stuck with the Twinkie again."

We sat in silence, noshing on our junky confections.

"I have never worked in a building with such an unhealthy vending machine," Al offered with mock revulsion. "I mean, really. Who eats pork rinds and fake onion rings at work? Yeech!"

"Says the man through a mouthful of Twinkie," I countered.

Al pulled out his phone and began scrolling. "I want to show you something," he said. I looked at the screen, noting a 360 degree view of a charming dining room with checkered tablecloths and colored Italian lights on the ceiling. "What's this?" I asked.

"It's called 'Bella.' It just opened. The chef is supposedly from Milan, dude."

I was silent.

"How would you like to go to dinner there with me? How about Friday, right after work?"

I paused. I felt stunned. "Al..." I began.

"Yes, dude."

"Al, this is just not a good time for me. My mother just died and I'm not up for a relationship right now."

"Dude, who's talking relationships? I'm just talking about trying a new restaurant."

I still hesitated. "This isn't some weird set-up where you're really married with three kids or something, is it?"

"No, I'm just a slacker bachelor, as advertised, face value. And don't worry. I don't like you either, dude!"

"Okay, I'll go with you. But on one condition."

"What's that?"

"That we don't talk about work at all."

"Dude, don't worry! We don't even talk about work AT work!"

He had a definite point.

That evening I decided to look up reviews on "Bella." I also wanted an idea of the price range because I definitely wanted to go dutch. My laptop was acting up lately so I reached into my purse for my cell phone. When I brought my phone out, I froze.

There it was. Another purple post-it note, sticking to the screen of my phone. I sank shakily into a chair at the kitchen table to read it.

In my mother's inimitable script, it simply read:

DON'T GO.
LOVE,
MAMA

I looked up at the ceiling as if the answer might be there. What was my mother doing?

On Thursday, the day before our dinner out, Al was surprisingly scarce. I could see him in Jeremy's office through the glass, eyes heavy as Jeremy gesticulated at a spreadsheet. He seemed to finally be working with no time for upside-down glasses or junk food runs...

On Friday morning, I dipped into my purse for my car key to commence my commute to the office. With my key came a large, folded sheet of very high-quality writing paper. My heart was thrumming a mile a minute as I unfolded it at the steering wheel of my car. It read:

> DON'T GO.
> NOT SAFE.
> LOVE,
> MAMA

In desperation, I looked up at the ceiling of my car. "Mama," I pleaded. "What's not safe? Is Al not safe?" Could it be that Al was not the genial goof that he appeared to be at work?

I sighed heavily, knowing that only one course of action was appropriate.

Al took my notice of cancelation well. I felt a tinge of guilt because he was clearly dressed up far more than usual today in a slick double-breasted suit with a maroon silk tie. He didn't even ask me why I wasn't going to dinner with him but said he would call me that evening.

That evening I sat in my sweatpants on the couch having chicken soup in front of the TV, lamenting my decision and wondering what gourmet offering I was missing to have a lousy bowl of soup alone. My cell phone displayed 9:30 PM. Just as I looked at it, the phone rang.

"Hello?"

"Dude!' Al sounded breathless. "Turn on the TV right now –channel 58!'

Without a word, I put the phone on speaker and switched away from the "I Love Lucy" rerun I was watching to behold a screen full of police cars, their lights churning frenetically in the darkness.

"Where is this?" I asked Al, but I already knew.

"Dude, how did you know we shouldn't go? The chef apparently snapped *after a fight with a disgruntled employee and shot up the place! Eight gravely injured and two fatalities!'*

As Al said this, the coroner's van came into view on screen.

I sighed deeply, reaching for my purse and removing my mother's notes. I smoothed them out on the coffee table in front of me.

"Want to come over, Al?"

"Sure."

"Please be careful, Al."

As I hung up, I not only felt gratitude once again for my mother's continued presence in my life but also pride because I sounded just like her in that moment.

HOMEGOING

Jenny sat on the porch steps of the small adobe-style house looking up at the moon rising over the cactus-speckled hills. The man was inside watching television. It was a show where a couple named Ralph and Alice strutted about their modest apartment hurling barbs at each other in loud, clipped tones. The man would watch, beady-eyed through the haze of one cigarette after another. He would occasionally cackle, usually only at something Ralph said and usually followed by a congested, croupy coughing spell.

Jenny liked these television nights because the man let her leave the room and sit outside, about twelve feet away. Normally she would have been fascinated or at the least interested by television because her parents didn't have one yet at home. Jenny valued time away from the man and would periodically look over her shoulder at the television set. The man would also quickly glance over his shoulder at her.

Jenny genuinely didn't know where she was. She remembered a long, bumpy, progressively hotter trip blindfolded in the trunk with the man periodically grabbing her by the arm or even by the hair to drink lukewarm, musty water from a metal cup. Then the trunk would slam shut and the bumpy miles continued until they arrived at the small adobe home in the middle of the desert. No neighbors, no school, no parties, no friends (too bad a cactus couldn't be a friend), no after-school milkshakes...just HIM and the endless desert, 24 hours a day. What did a 15 year-old girl and a 50 year-old man have in common anyway, Jenny wondered as the Ralph character bellowed, "To the moon, Alice, to the moon!" to bawdy laughter from the studio audience and the man.

Jenny looked at the moon, thinking her chances of going there tonight or going home to her parents were exactly the same – zero.

Jenny knew this was it. She would die tonight. She was going home to her parents. She was going to the moon.

The dreadlocked, perpetually humming housekeeper had just left Jenny's room after mopping the green linoleum floor around her bed, giving it a translucent sheen. Jenny looked down at her withered arms. They reminded her of dried corn husks. She wished she could shed her skin. She saw her swollen, purple toes poking out beneath the blanket and was repulsed that something so ugly could be part of her. Her breathing felt tight and painful on inhalation.

The nurse arrived and checked Jenny's identification bracelet, reading it aloud. "Jennifer, would you like to watch TV before we get you ready for the night?" The nurse picked up the remote and flipped past an infomercial and a mega-church service. She stopped flipping as the screen settled on a black-and-white interior of a modest apartment.

"Oh, it's one of those old black-and-white shows! You might enjoy that!" the nurse said with a cheerful lilt.

And there it was.

Just as Jenny remembered it. Ralph and Alice, looking as they did all those years ago! The droll neighbor with the porkpie hat popping in to complicate things! The canned laughter! The loud, clipped bickering echoed across the decades exactly as she remembered it! Here it was again, in crisp black-and-white. Then Ralph curled his fist at Alice on the screen and delivered his signature line to the delighted laughter of the long-dead audience.

"To the moon, Alice, to the moon!" Jenny said in tandem with the TV in a dry, papery, wispy voice. It was the very last thing she would say aloud.

The nurse turned around. "Oh, honey. I'm not Alice. I'm Demetria. I'll be taking care of you tonight."

Jenny turned her head away from the TV toward her window. The moon was rising over the sign for the "Cactus Hills Care Center." The loneliness and longing of many years came crashing down upon her. She was going home – to her parents, to the moon. But questions loomed in her mind:

Will they recognize me?

Will they remember me?

Will they still love me?

Jenny's last breath hurt greatly on inhalation but ended on a quiet, peaceful exhalation as the answer came to her:

Of course they will.

POEMS

POLICE WORK

Flashlight beams
Crossing in the woods
As boots crunch on
Last year's leaves
A hoarse cacophony
Of barks and voices
And then
A small corner of
Bright blue peeking
Out from the forest
Floor detritus
Last seen by human
Eyes
Just this morning
At a quiet bus stop

ARREST

Arrest
Ceasing, ending
Handcuffs roughly
In the
Shape of
Infinity

THE SPIRIT OF 9-11-01

Under quiet, empty blue skies
Much like my grandfather
Would have experienced in
Youth
Our collective heart lay in
A crater
Deeper than the one left
By the towers
Strangers held doors, greeted
One another and said
"Thank you"
No partisans here
Just Americans
No red, no blue

Where is the spirit of 9/11 when we need it most?

JESUIT RECRUITS: FUTURE SOLDIERS

The thumbnail photos
Show young men laughing
And back-slapping in
Their prime
These look like tanned
Frat boys
But, most assuredly, they
Are not
These are the future
Soldiers
In God's Army

Ordination is many years
Away
Some will not make it
Bowed down by the
Passage of time, doubts
And diligence
But the photos show
Only hope, possibility
And the radiance of youth

TO A CHILD, DISAPPEARED

You look out at me
From just beneath the Domino's coupons
Last seen on 5/10/83
You might be starting to comb grey
Hair about now
Or maybe you are in darkness
After all of the raw shouting
Your eyes are clear and confident
You
Are
Safe and warm
In the past

SUMMER-WINTER NIGHT

My mother dubbed it "Summer-Winter night"
That first warm night in
Early spring
We would gather
My mother, my brother and I
Always in my girlhood room

We walked about our dreams
And plans
The sweet night air
Refreshing our faces
The sky
A vast portfolio
Of
Stars

DREAMS

(AUTHOR'S NOTE: Lucid dreaming has been reported to be on the rise since the COVID-19 outbreak. I can personally attest to that! The following pages are dreams I have had during the pandemic. I have made every effort to record each dream exactly as I remember it. Logical incongruities abound, but, after all, these are dreams. Only my subconscious can take credit as the real author).

FOUND

I stood at a railing
On a bridge
Over a river
I was writing something
I know not what

A sudden gruff voice
A cacophony of stamping
Feet around me
"There he is!" said gruff voice, finger jabbed
At the water below

Then I saw a man's legs
In the water
Clad in custodian-green
Work pants

I was invisible then but
I knew to move out of
The way
My blue notebook still
Balanced on the railing

“I got ‘em” bellowed
Gruff voice
Although other dark
Uniformed figures were
Working in a flurry of
Reaching

The man in custodian-green pants
Was pulled ingloriously over the
Bridge railing
Where he landed
Feet flapping over his
Head
With a hard thwack

Still invisible
I saw his (also) custodian-green
Jacket
His face pale, eyes closed
No bruising, blackening
Or bloating
His sandy hair falling
Away from his face in
Symmetrical shards
No doubt a precision
Haircut getting a little
Long
(How did his hair dry so quickly?)
His neatly trimmed
Mustache
Recalled a friend’s husband of
Long ago

4/11/20

UP IN FLAMES

My husband Bob and I were hiking in a woods with a friend of ours who had seen a rare type of hawk in a farm field earlier. The three of us were exiting the woods and the unplanted farm field was at our right side. My friend's back was to me and I could see her head angle to the right with interest as a small speck high in the sky became larger and less distant. As it came closer, what I expected to be a hawk was actually a drone of some sort. However, as it came even closer, it turned on its side and then abruptly pulled back, as if startled (and startling us)! I then saw it was a space ship or UFO of some sort. It smoothly landed in the field and promptly exploded into flames.

As we walked away, I also noted a semi-truck burning at the edge of the field. A man stood calmly and a bit too closely to the truck with his hands on a young girl's shoulders in a fatherly pose. Another man stood alone, very close to the flaming truck. He waved to us and smiled with no urgency. His body language showed no intent of leaving.

4-17-20

DOCTORS WITHOUT BOUNDARIES

My husband Bob and I were splitting our residences between our old apartment on Miner Street in Milwaukee and my childhood home in Hales Corners. One night we were locked out of the apartment so we went home to Hales Corners. We hadn't been there in a while. It was about 3 AM.

When I stepped into the darkened family room, I had the uneasy feeling that we were not alone.

"Hello?!" I called out.

Several seconds later an outdoor light came on, illuminating the bushes under the front window.

The next thing I knew, a doctor in full PPE was coming down the stairs into the family room. He sported goggles, a face shield and the ubiquitous yellow gown.

"Hello, I'm Susan Knier, a speech-language pathologist from Ascension All Saints Hospital in Racine." My professional instincts kicked in remarkably despite the fact that I was startled and irritated by his presence. "Before that, I worked at Aurora St. Luke's in Milwaukee for 26 years," I added.

"I'm one of those, too," the doctor said.

"What are you doing here?" I asked.

"I'm staying here," he replied. "You know, I've done it before for a couple nights. Others have been here, too."

Doctors squatting at my house?! I was incredulous.

"If you need a place tonight, there's an open bedroom," the doctor went on. "I don't have the girls tonight."

He showed us to the open bedroom, which turned out to be my girlhood room. I was startled and even a bit irritated that the doctor's girls had apparently made their own décor. A white board was decorated in various colors with "Super Sisters!" written at the top. The bedclothes smelled of strangers.

We slept. The next morning the house was perfectly quiet and empty. Apparently the doctor was busy saving lives at St. Luke's.

4/18/20

YOU CAN GO HOME AGAIN...OR CAN YOU? OR: AIRBORNE! ALOFT!

"Woodwork is original, door handles are solid pewter," intoned the realtor in his sonorous baritone but slightly monotonous voice. The realtor and a strapping, square-jawed 35 year-old man stood on the balcony overlooking the palatial living room with a cathedral ceiling, intricate floor to ceiling windows and hardwood floors as blond as the prospective buyer's hair.

Suddenly, the prospective buyer said, "I'm the kid that used to do this!" and vaulted expertly over the balcony railing, falling a great distance to the blond wood floor below. He landed almost perfectly, with only a small stutter step backward, legs apart and arms arced upward toward the shocked realtor in a classic showman's pose. The man lifted his broad, clefted chin to the massive ceiling and his blue eyes glimmered with satisfaction.

(The dream ends here, but imagine the realtor's surprise on two points: First, witnessing an unexpected and potentially lethal stunt that he had seen on TV many years ago by this same person. Second, the irony of a former child actor poised to buy the very home in which many scenes of his 1980s TV series were shot...)

4-25-20

FLOOD STAGE

A boy and his father drowned in their van as flood waters swept them away down the street.

The last sighting reported was of the boy frantically using a toy steering wheel in the back seat – as futile as his father's efforts in using the real wheel as a wall of water curled and descended on them.

Street names in the area were later re-named for dogs as the boy loved animals.

5-11-20

THE GRAND UNCLE

Apparently I had a grand uncle on my mother's side of the family that I had never heard of or met. He wanted to get everyone together at a party at his house. He had been a big-deal CEO of a reputable but relatively obscure business back in the 1950s through the early 1970s. I honestly wondered how he could still be alive.

On the day of the party, I arrived at his huge home with a cold 12-pack of beer in my hand. I somehow knew to go down to the basement to store it away. The basement was huge and empty, except for an alcove in which an ancient wooden "ice box" resided. I pushed back the warped cabinet door to see a mountain of ice. I pulled a beer from the 12-pack and opened up what looked like a cellar door. In the dim light, I could see countless cases of beer and liquor. I placed my 11-pack in there, thinking I needn't have bothered.

At that point, the Grand Uncle bounded down the stairs into the basement, charging around the huge perimeter in vigorous laps. "Hello, Susan!" he called out in a hale, hardy voice.

I found my way through to what used to be his home office. A large group of millennials were seated on the sofas, visiting quietly. I couldn't help but think that this home office was bigger than most apartments! I stopped at the Grand Uncle's desk. All vestiges of his work had been removed – no phone, no blotter, no in-basket. All that remained was a swivel chair and an immaculate surface. Right next to the desk was a single bed, beautifully made with an overstuffed pillow.

My cousin appeared at my side as we gazed at the Grand Uncle's desk and then at the bed in close proximity. "He must have been such a hard worker," she reflected.

5-13-20

I WANT YOUR LICENSE

A woman of about 35 years of age with dishwater blond hair tucked neatly behind her ears appeared beside me at an undisclosed location.

"Excuse me, can I have your driver's license?" she asked pleasantly. "I can pay."

"My driver's license?"

"Yes," she said, as if it was the most routine request in the world.

My mind was fraught with questions that for some reason I did not air. For instance, why? She was much younger than I and we did not resemble one another one bit. If I did this, could I get into some sort of trouble? Instead, I asked, "How much?"

She leaned back and pulled out a large wad of bills in a taut roll. "Well," she said, casually. "Payroll. About $3,000. I could go up to $5,000."

I was paralyzed in speech, action and decision-making. Why didn't I ask the real questions?

5-15-20

CATCHING A FLIGHT

I was arriving for a flight. At the "airport," I stuck my head into a room that resembled a semi-darkened movie theater. Flight attendants were ushering people out of the theater after waving them out of their seats. The flight attendants wore shiny navy blouses with beanies that were the same shiny navy with a patch of hot pink. They were using a "thumbs up" signal to one another as they called and identified customers. One of the flight attendants was seated and emphatically gave a two "thumbs up."

I left the theater and noticed another flight attendant next door at the entrance to what appeared to be a flight bridge. I half expected her to chastise me for "skipping" the "thumbs up" process in the "theater" but instead she was very friendly and readily took my proffered passport. She then retrieved a clipboard and completed some paperwork. "It'll be $60.31," she stated, circling the number.

"Wow, that's really cheap," I remarked.

Her tone remained friendly and cheerful but the flight attendant retorted, "You think so?" Then she shifted gears: "Follow me and I'll get you prepped for your flight." I obediently followed her down the flight bridge.

Minutes later I was seated on the plane, adjusting and tightening the head band on my face shield.

Will air travel ever be the same? Will it be as strange as a dream?

5-16-20

NO ONE IS FEEDING THE CAT

We were living in my old childhood home in Hales Corners. My mother was there in the family room, looking like she was in her 40s or 50s.

I noticed that the cat's food and water bowls were gone but the cat was still there. I picked her up. She was fur and bones – just like I remembered her looking and feeling before she died in my real life three years ago.

"Mom, where's the cat's food and water? When did someone last feed the cat?" I was alarmed suddenly that I'd been too busy to notice. The cat was surprisingly content and wide-eyed in my arms.

My mother seemed busy and distracted, re-arranging things in the room. "I don't know," she shrugged indifferently.

Then we were packed into a car. I was sandwiched in the back seat between two strangers. In the front seat, an unknown driver sat aside the cat with my mother in the passenger seat.

I was now desperate. "We have got to get the cat something to eat," I pleaded. The cat's head bowed down in the front seat. I could see a bone protruding right under the fur.

The stranger to my left slowly produced what looked like a cat treat from his inside jacket pocket – just one small treat. It seemed to take him forever to hand it up to the anonymous driver. The driver accepted the treat and gazed at it dumbly between his fingers. The cat continued on contentedly in the seat beside him, neither one moving to do anything.

5-20-20

TERRIFIED

I was getting onto an elevator. On the way in, I accidentally but lightly bumped the arm of the passenger departing the elevator car. As most would, I murmured "Sorry."

Then, after I had pressed my floor, the passenger quickly turned and re-entered the elevator with me after doing a double-take look at me.

The elevator door closed. He looked at me with hazel eyes, slightly averted. His hair was brown with blond streaks and very wavy with a long bang skewed to one side, almost like what we used to call a "New Wave" haircut. I estimated him to be in his early twenties. (As of this writing, I am 55 years old).

"Is there a way to put this thing on hold?" he said, somewhat coldly.

I hesitated, realizing that there probably was a hold button on the elevator control panel. But this stranger was still looking at me, somewhat askance but ominously. I did not feel like being helpful in his request as I considered the implications of being "on hold" with this passenger. My only offense was lightly bumping into him.

Then I woke up.

7-1-20

"OH, LOOK! THEY'RE LEAVING!"

I was walking in an unnamed mall when I saw what looked like a ladies' clothing and jewelry boutique behind glass. Unlike most stores in the mall, the glass was loaded with so many sales decals that it was difficult to see inside. I also noted that a narrow glass door (closed on the mall side) was the only entry point. I calculated that I had approximately ten minutes to look around the store before I needed to drive my 38-mile commute to the hospital in Racine to see one of my outpatient speech therapy clients.

I went into the store and looked briefly and noncommittally at scarves, sweaters and blouses. I noticed a table devoted to miscellaneous jewelry and I absently picked up a bracelet with various colored, almost translucent beads.

There were two clerks in the store, both elderly women. One had been folding handkerchiefs and scarves at a nearby table. She walked over to me and smiled sweetly with her arms crossed behind her back as I looked at the bracelet.

"Handcrafted," she said simply. "From India."

As I nodded at her and replaced the bracelet in its box, I saw a woman at the store's entry door. She seemed to be struggling. "I can't get the door open," she said, her volume escalating with alarm. "Can I get some help here?"

The two clerks shrugged at each other. The clerk that had interacted with me said in a dull tone, "I suppose we could call someone in the mall..." But then she went back to folding handkerchiefs.

I walked over to the entry door where my fellow customer was furiously pulling at the door knob and alternately rapping equally furiously on the door. The door was so heavily decaled that we couldn't have gotten the attention of someone in the mall corridor if we had stood on our heads.

The woman stopped struggling with the door. Her complexion was scarlet with a mix of fear and frustration, her fists furled at her sides. "There must be another door in this place!" she cried, more to herself than to me. I followed her to the back wall of the store where there was indeed another door. It was of scarred, gunmetal grey steel with no knob or handle. The woman began pounding on this door with two open palms. The pounding had a hollow, reverberating tone. She began then to crouch down, alternately pounding and placing her ear to the door to detect any activity on the other side. She did not directly communicate with me but continued to probe various parts of the door.

I walked back over to where the elderly clerk had stood folding handkerchiefs a few minutes ago, but her task was apparently completed and only an empty cardboard box remained on the table.

Then, from behind me, another voice said in a startled tone, "Oh, look! They're leaving! They're getting out!"

I ran back over to the steel door, hoping my window of opportunity to escape had not somehow passed. A line of customers was descending onto metal stairs and into darkness. The walkway resembled a tunnel with sides of sheet metal but no top. We walked quietly but breathlessly.

Inexplicably, we came out of the tunnel onto an unpaved rural road that appeared to bisect a farm. I looked back to see the black peaks of the mall roof almost level with the earth, as if the entire structure was underground. I had no idea where the parking lot that contained my car might be as I looked down the rural highway.

All I knew for certain was that I had an outpatient 38 miles away in Racine in about 25 minutes.

10-31-20

SOCIALLY DISTANCED, EVEN IN NATURE

I was walking across a large, open meadow when I noticed an owl in the shadows on the ground underneath the generous bough of an old fir tree that bordered the meadow. Hmm, I thought. Owls don't usually perch on the ground. But as my gaze expanded to see what was in front of me I realized that this was far from the most unusual sight this day.

In front of me was a line of wild animals, each gazing at me with preternatural calm and stillness. A squirrel stood calmly next to a chipmunk who was next to a woodchuck who was then next to a deer. The squirrel stood stock still in the middle of a small rotted tree stump.

What struck me most was that each animal was exactly six feet apart from the other.

The animals are doing it, too! Social distancing! My heart began to race. The animals continued to calmly stare at me. I was about six feet away from the center of the line. My husband used to marvel at my ability to closely attract animals in nature, dubbing it the "St. Francis effect." I had never been afraid of an animal before. Suddenly, I became fearful and decided to leave. I slowly turned around and walked away in careful, measured steps. I could hear the grass rustling gently against my shoes as I thought, "Why aren't they afraid of me?"

Then I heard another rustling sound in back of me. Apparently, almost as soon as I turned around, the animals scattered and left.

11-27-20

THE ROCK CONCERT

It was impossibly great to be with mom again, considering she had passed away on 9-25-20. We were at an outdoor rock concert with my husband Bob, sitting high up on metal bleachers. I wondered in passing how we had gotten mom up there, considering that she had significantly difficulty walking over the past several years and was almost immobile just prior to death. Oh, well. We were here – together again!

Mom leaned against me. She was wearing her favorite sweater, a cheap robin's egg blue cardigan I had bought for her at WalMart years ago. I put my arm around her frail but warm frame.

"It's so good to see you, Susan," she said.

"Good to see you again, too, mom," I replied.

Our eyes moved to the stage below. The concert was about to begin. The performer was apparently a "one-man band." He was a tall, string-bean thin fellow wearing a battered black top hat. He reminded me slightly of Todd Rundgren in his heyday. He wielded the microphone and addressed the audience in a lazy baritone. "Okay, ladies and gentlemen, we'll be getting to the loud stuff later."

I flinched slightly, wondering how mom would tolerate the "loud stuff." But the performer took a seat behind the drum kit and began a set of rather soft, "singer-songwriter"-type material.

Jump cut to me sitting alone on an adjacent bleacher. The performer seemed to be on break. I stood up, wondering where mom and Bob had gone. I climbed down from the bleachers and scanned the parking lot. Then I saw mom in the distance in her beloved blue cardigan, walking like Gumby but still miraculously walking without her walker! Bob was standing near her next to a large white sedan.

I ran toward them. By the time I reached the parking lot, mom was buckled inside the white sedan. Bob stood calmly with his arms folded on the roof of the driver's side.

"Hey," I said, breathlessly. "Where are you guys going?"

Bob rolled his eyes. "SOMEBODY here got TIRED and wanted to go home IMMEDIATELY!" he intoned, winking and smiling at me.

The only unanswered question was how would I have gotten home?

11-26-20

THE REFRIGERATOR

Mom called me on her vacation. "Susan, you have got to see the refrigerator where I'm staying. It's wonderful! I want you to see it!"

I pulled into the gas station parking lot on my scooter. Apparently mom's vacation lodging was attached to the side of the mini-mart portion of the gas station. It was not exactly where I expected mom to be vacationing, but she had sounded happy and enthusiastic on the phone.

I entered the mini-mart as a bell rang above the door. I noticed a small indoor corral for bikes and scooters. Unusual, but I liked the idea. A clerk stood several feet away with her back to me stocking cigarettes into various brand-specific compartments on the wall.

"Excuse me," I said. "Can I bring my scooter in and park it here?"

"Sure," she replied noncommittally and without turning around.

Once the scooter was secured, I located the door to mom's vacation rental off the mini-mart. I knocked on the battered brown door. It opened almost immediately. There was mom in her beloved blue cardigan, beaming at me and gripping her walker.

I stepped inside and she greeted me warmly. A dimly lit and very narrow corridor lay ahead. It looked almost too narrow to accommodate us, but mom led me ahead with urgency in her tone of voice and in her step.

“Come on, Susan,” she exhorted. “You have got to see the refrigerator in this place. It’s wonderful. I’ve never seen one like it before!”

I was beginning to share her excitement as I looked into her gleaming eyes in the semi-darkness.

“Well, mom,” I replied. “Maybe I’ll be buying you a new refrigerator soon!”

11-27-20

ACKNOWLEDGMENTS AND DEDICATIONS

To my wonderful husband, Bob Knier! What a gem! You listened to every word of this book.

To my beloved parents, Rosemary and Gene Mahoney. You are my role models for kindness, writing and art. I miss you both terribly.

To my caring in-laws, Bernie and Ted Knier. You live the Golden Rule.

To God. You have shown me great mercy over the past 56 years.